Sincerely Yours Forever, C.S.

By, Cheyenne Sioux

To Kim,

Thank you so so much!

Cheyenne Sioux ♡

For the ones who encouraged me to pursue my dreams

and the one I am over the moon for.

Sincerely Yours Forever, C.s.

Cheyenne Sioux

cheyennesiouxpoetry@gmail.com

ISBN: 9798377948667

Printed in the United States of America

This poetry collection does not come with a table of contents.

Please feel free to read in the order you desire.

Enjoy the adventure of your read!
I hope it's a magical one.

"I am made up of fragments of poetry glued together hoping one day to become art."

Tragic is the girl

who stops building her castle

just because another

doesn't believe

she holds the power to reign.

You needed the moon
but I was starlight

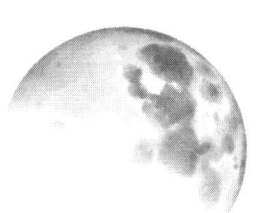

and we got comfortable
in the delusion

that we were something
other than two strangers

looking for the same way
to escape our lonely hearts.

Cheyenne Sioux

Grasping at shards of the moon
I reluctantly seek
to find a way
to numb the quake in my chest.

If for nothing but to stop
the reflecting

of all the disappointments
my soul does mirror back.

For, I am a walking disaster-
a catastrophic event,
                a time bomb ticking

at which the world awaits.

Holding its breath
for the next time I lose my way

and splinter and shatter...

Cheyenne Sioux

Like broken sea glass
scattered along the shoreline.

If only I were that lucky...
to be washed away by the nights tide.

But here I stay still grasping
at shards of the moon,
hoping one day

I'll hold its luminous glow
and finally, be set free.

Cheyenne Sioux

She mirrors back hope
as if stealing it from others
could pass as her own self-love.

If I stripped down my pretense
you would see into the hollow of my chest.

You would see the weight each word carries
as I hold in my deep breaths.

My mind clouds my vision,
like a vulture crooning to the pain

And I linger in this darkness
wondering if I will ever be the same?

This world has become heavy
emptiness tearing me by the seams

And I fight to awaken the soul
that had built a world filled with dreams.

If I stripped down my pretense
you would never look at me the same

For the girl who always smiles
is fighting for her happiness to remain.

Cheyenne Sioux

Poetry is fumbling locks and sweaty palms.

It's crumbled paper in the corner
as you try to breathe through
emotion and heart
and decipher what resides in your soul.

It's fragrant feelings fluttering
on whimsical desire and plagiarizing pain
that seeps in to steal your joy.

It's the sediments shifting
dawn breaking-
releasing
blood sweat and tears to the world

and hoping this battle
was not in vain.

That these words would
touch another's heart

and they to, will unlock the door
no longer afraid of being slain.

Cheyenne Sioux

This may feel like the end of the world
but you are one heartbreak closer
to becoming the very best version of you.

Hang in there,
for light comes to relieve the darkness
and shadows disappear when hit by the sun.

Cheyenne Sioux

Afternoon phone calls
landlines and vinyl tabletops
take me back in time.

A film reels in the background
yet I'm hanging on your every word.

My heart on display
I poured it out for you,
never knew,
I was getting leftover love.

Never knew it was her scent
hanging on your skin.

Maple in your hair
tousled from hands
that was not my own.

You smile at me
while you think of her

Cheyenne Sioux

and I sit here
swimming in the sea of your eyes

Oblivious

that your heart is beating
to a different tune

and I'm just your B-side romance

an in-between of clarity
on a Sunday afternoon.

Cheyenne Sioux   15

She grows tired of
upholding appearances

squinting and batting eyes
at the sun.

Her soul wishes to rest,
to be devoured by
the dark side of the moon.

Where solace carries her
into her dreams
and midnight falcon's fly

Where she can be nothing
but starlight twinkling
across an endless sky.

Cheyenne Sioux

Sincerely Yours Forever, C.s.

How easy it is to lose ourselves
wading knee-deep in the conceptions
of who others choose for us to be.

I grow tired of the restlessness

of not fully being me.

Cheyenne Sioux

Falling leaves dance in the rearview mirror
as I'm losing myself on these upstate roads.

Radio dialed to a volume of seven
I'm singing in nothing but off-key notes.

My fingers trace the passenger window
in the spot our initials used to be
from that distant autumn morning
when you first said you were in love with me.

Rewind me back to that moment
when the world seemed to spin just right
when love wasn't just a moment
that would diminish in an afternoon's light.

Back to the times, you tucked your fingers
in the pockets of my sweaters
when you said that everything of mine
was better.

I swore then, this love would be ours forever.
But now I sit here and just remember

Cheyenne Sioux

Every moment laughs turned to tears
and seasons were no longer a greeting.

When the warmth in your voice
turned to frost-bitten speech
I could've sworn my heart stopped beating.

Nothing was wrong, nothing was right
just blinded by romanticized light,
we learned it all too well.

Now, I miss those autumn drives
when leaves danced in our rearview
and we had nothing but time

But I'll always remember
all too well that you were once mine.

Cheyenne Sioux

This love was an unrehearsed play
fumbling and stepping on toes.

We never matched up to the same rhythm
and this is how heartbreak goes.

Act one was butterflies and daisy filled dreams
while foreshadows loomed -
not everything is how it seems.

For act two came about and it was
love at first sight we were blinded
underneath infatuations light.

Act three was a cold one
it numbed me to the core.
For something had changed
and you weren't mine anymore.

Now I stand center stage, alone in act four
perfecting my improv, settling the score.
pretending it's all part of the show

when underneath this performance
I'm willing myself to let you go.

Cheyenne Sioux

We were too young to be
handing out broken hearts
as party favors.

Bandaging our minds
from words inflicted
without a thought
to the malice beneath them.

How does one learn
the true meaning of love
with nothing but hatred
plaguing their heart
and spilling off their tongue?

We must do better – *be better*

So that kids aren't growing up
with a damaged perception
and mistaking love for
growing pains.

Cheyenne Sioux 21

I

Lips bruised by his words
every promise laced with lies.

Like venom from a snake
they pierced her heart
it bleeds, she cries.

A wildfire spreading
through her veins-
ignites her soul.

She longs for a love
that keeps her safe
and makes her whole.

II

Lips bruised by his words
heart bleeding from his lies.

She is shattered from the pain
and no one hears her cries.

Another drop of blood
she sheds yet again
and the knife of his love
plunged deeper within.

Her soul is barely hanging
by a thread of who she was.
For he has ruined the girl
he swore that he loves.

Cheyenne Sioux

My evergreen heart faded
for the first time
shriveled beneath autumns
sauntering embrace.

It arrived at my doorstep
when it should've been you
but somehow the seasons
have taken your place.

You had said this is what
forever should feel like
and then was gone in a blink of an eye.

I guess I was something
to leave behind this year
because forever turned into goodbye.

Cheyenne Sioux

I knew I was in trouble
when you left
with the pieces of my heart
and I remained
with nothing but an echo.

Cheyenne Sioux

Anxiousness blooms
a garden of thorns in my chest
an embroidered ribcage
with vines of bated breath.

Hallowed my heart
I've succumbed to the pain
alone in this darkness
where no light shall remain.

My mind beckons;
a raven shedding its oaken voice;
for release from this prison
yet I am given no choice.

Haunted by the ghosts
of who I'm told to be
when all I ever wanted
was to be imperfectly me.

Cheyenne Sioux

Invisibility cast itself upon my shoulders
like a cloak choosing its queen.
But who wishes to be among the shadows
never being seen?

Cheyenne Sioux

I twisted my words into a bow
so, they would always be presented
with beauty and ease.

But sentiments are not always sentimental
and people are not always easy to please.

My words now shadow me
a ribboning veil of invisibility
and I fracture beneath the weight.

Spinning into still silence
no one seems to notice my absence
and no one seems to care.

The world carousels around me
and it's as if I'm not even there.

I am but a convenient thought
when the time feels right, *when I'm needed*

but where does everyone disappear
when I need them in return?

Cheyenne Sioux   28

Sincerely Yours Forever, C.s.

I'm hyperventilating through the motions

the constant back and forth

jumping up and down

waving my hands

as I shout to the sky.

But no one notices me.

The world bustles on

people keep fading

and I'm still standing here

wrapped in this cloak

Praying for the day

I no longer care who sees me.

Cheyenne Sioux   29

I am sentimental so I walk in the rain
let the earth's tears wash over me
and cleanse away my pain.

I am sentimental so I dance when the music ends
let the melody course through my veins
where my soul and passion blends.

I am sentimental so I write the words I feel
I dress them up nicely like a band aid
needed to heal.

This is my rain, this is my dance,
this may be the only chance –

I'll ever have to explain
the reason I wait to walk in the rain.

Cheyenne Sioux

I am still learning

to love the shards of myself

that never made it to the light.

— I'll find beauty in my brokenness.

We orbited like the sun and moon

never coming close

just caught in a moment

of serendipity

we shone a light

on each other's hearts

and unleashed the stars

hidden within.

We were catastrophic

two comets creating *stardust*

from our collision

Cheyenne Sioux 33

She wanted someone to know her
not simply who she was on the surface
but to plunge deeply into the vaults
of her mind

where broken dreams reside
and forgotten memories live on.

She wanted someone
who would dust away the cobwebs

and love her through the darkness
while she found her inner light.

Cheyenne Sioux

You want to step into the role
you think you're finally ready?

I should go ahead and warn you
I'm a little unsteady.

For you have big shoes to fill
my imagination ran wild

for its hard to cope
with the absence of a parent
as a hurting child.

You were the first to show me
that some wounds don't heal

and that some love will
never truly be real.

No matter that I tried to convince
myself otherwise

it all just piled up into your mountain of lies.

I don't expect you to understand
I don't expect you to care.

For how can you feel remorse

when through the pain
you were never there?

Cheyenne Sioux

Don't let the pain
change your heart

It's too *magical* of a place

to let someone blind
to its beauty

steal away with its grace.

Cheyenne Sioux

I etched your name

into my paper-thin heart

hoping you would stay awhile.

Now the thought of you,

is a slow drift

Between the moments

taken for sleep to carry me away.

I built castle walls
upon empty promises.

Swung my sword
swiftly through your lies.

And when you spoke of me

as if I was nothing

I straightened my crown

and simply walked away.

One day you will see me reign.

I pressed peonies between
the pages of my notebooks
to remind me what *loving you*
will always feel like.

One day you will find a love
so powerful it shatters the stars.

And beneath the falling starlight
you will find why your heart
endured so much pain.

So many late-night wishes
to a darkened sky –

Only to wake to disappointment.

For it is among the brokenness
when all hope seems lost
the most beautiful things form

And galaxies are created.

Cheyenne Sioux

I have outgrown the girl I used to be
falling in love so carelessly.

I no longer waste flower petals
on trivial he loves me; he loves me nots
mimicking the idea of what counts as love.

For I will stop chasing the wind
and wait for the answer to come from above.

Cheyenne Sioux   41

Like a potion crafted
to reawaken my soul
I absorb the light of a thousand stars

Each twinkle travels
to the depths of every
dark crevice of my being.

Reforming the broken pieces
and restoring the air to my lungs.

I am no longer a dying shell
gasping for a sliver of oxygen
to meet my lips

I merely exist among the clouds
not bound by time
or gravity

            or even *love.*

Just delicately floating like a feather
swept away in the wind.

Cheyenne Sioux

Cracks within the sediment

fills with your stretching *roots*

Shift your focus to the sun

it only gets brighter from *here.*

Cheyenne Sioux   43

Echoes of my life
are woven into the stars
like street lamps flickering
to illuminate my path.

I travel to familiar places
searching for a way to
feel at home again.

Swallowing back the lump
in my throat,

        I smile.

Reminiscing the time lost,
moments I thought I'd never
set foot in again.

But this time the pain lessens.

I shed the agony that encased
my heart in vines

and feel the flutter
as it beats freely at last.

I let raindrops kiss my skin,
the sun's rays melt into my core,
a vibrant warmth healing me.

Unfurling my petals,
I am blooming into bliss

holding hands with my past
once more as I let go
and extend my hand to the future.

The stars are street-lamps
guiding me towards the moment
the sun rises and

I flourish.

a sunflower among wildflowers
no longer withering to all that I left behind.

Cheyenne Sioux   45

Encased in her cocoon she knew
it was time to break free
even if she became a moth
she would flutter her wings
beautifully.

Don't fret if your petals
still remain cocooned shut

and the rain still droplets
onto your leaves

whilst the sun remains out of focus
playing peek-a-boo with the clouds.

For it is all part of the process
and one day, you will flourish
in that golden sunlight.

But be patient,
for flowers need time to bloom.

Cheyenne Sioux   47

She is searching for the wild in her soul

the phenomenon of existing -

vastly, freely, and confidently.

She realized though people may leave
it wasn't a reflection of her heart.

It was merely the end of their season together
much like a sunrise is sent to relieve the darkness

some people walk with us through the pain
until we find our way back to the light.

Cheyenne Sioux

When Someone Asks Me "Am I Supposed to Feel Something?"

I think of morning light gleaming through my
windowpane as rainbows illuminate my skin and the
warmth of the sun radiates onto my face, electrifying my
eyes as they open
to a new day.

I think of the daisies in the field next door their fragrant
aroma beckoning me to come lay amidst them and ignore
responsibility.

I think of that simple, shy boy I have always loved and that
maybe today will be the day I am courageous enough to
tell him how I feel.

And the butterflies that awaken in my chest and flutter
about when our eyes meet and I lose my nerve all over
again.

I remember days that were simple hearing mom bustle
through the house to whip up my favorite breakfast and
holding the door for the elderly couple at the market –
who visited every Tuesday without fail.

I reminisce on these little moments, the small adventures
that shaped the person I was and helped me to grow into
the woman I am now.

And the only answer I have is yes, you are supposed to feel
something because feeling is one of the purest
forms of being alive.

It wasn't until I realized even the stars
form in darkness, and the flowers
endure the rain.

If they can weather a storm
I can survive a little pain.

- An ode to growth

Cheyenne Sioux 51

At last, the fog had lifted,
the vines loosened
and my heart was set free

to blush, blossom, and bloom

and I sprouted like a wildflower
ready to taste the sun.

Cheyenne Sioux

I studied my pollen dusted fingertips
with a smile wide across my face

Because I knew this was the moment
I had wished for in the first place.

I looked around me with freshly lit eyes
and I spread my hearts wings,
lifting towards the skies.

I had wished upon each wildflower
sprinkled in the field

And I realized finally,
my fate had been revealed.

It was but a glimpse
a moment passing by

But it showed me the way to courage
and the strength I needed to try.

Cheyenne Sioux   53

Sunlight spills across my skin
reminding me that every moment
I breathe is a gift to cherish.

That even stars have to turn to stardust
and fall from the sky.

But that doesn't mean they're lost
forever because they live on in the
souls of you and I.

Cheyenne Sioux

Flowers are love notes

to the *wild* in your soul.

I orchestrated a symphony
with each thrum of my hearts beat
as I crescendo into a new beginning.

This was my metamorphosis.

The moment I realized this cocoon
was not a trap meant to hold me.

I was not submitting to darkness
but forming, growing, emerging –

into a butterfly
soul-laced with starlight.

Upon revived wings, I soar
to the song that awoken

my slumbering heart.

Cheyenne Sioux

People always search for the truth in magic
but maybe – the point of it all is in the unknown.

Not what's discovered but what's felt
beneath the surface of every moment.

The small messages hidden within the stars
that awaken souls and help broken-winged
butterflies take flight.

Maybe we seek truth out of desperation
when the magic has been within us all along.

A butterfly cannot be caged
with stardust on her wings

I am pure reckoning magic
capable of incredible things.

No matter the shackles
you try and place upon my heart

I am free, uncaged, and wild
blushing and blooming

becoming art.

Cheyenne Sioux

When you are feeling discouraged
and your soul is needing rest
know that I am here to pick you up.

Know that I will stand by your side
and encourage you to find the strength.

You are loved, valued, needed.

Keep blooming this world needs
your rare beauty.

- a love note to yourself.

you are a sunflower.

dance with trees and befriend the bees

this journey was never meant to be lonely.

It's time to rise again.

Light a match within the dark crevices of your mind, body, soul and feel the warmth spill over you as it ignites. It's time to rekindle that inner light, to lift yourself from ash and rubble.

No more simmering embers waiting to be suffocated beneath a blanket of doubts, insecurities or failures. There is a spark flickering within you waiting to be lit.

You are not too broken; you are not too far gone.

Find that flicker and set your dreams ablaze.

You fear comets

yet you have never seen a girl

rise from simmering embers

and discover

she is still made of fire.

I'll send a smoke signal to my former self
and thank her for pressing on when the flames
had all but burnt out.

I daydream of a love
so unpredictable and free
as a sunflower refusing to stop
stretching to *kiss the sky*.

Cheyenne Sioux

Sincerely Yours Forever, C.s.

You are a golden ray
plucked straight from the sun

how lucky we are to experience your light.

He was that after-the-rain kind of feeling
the pause between guitar string hums,
subtle clues lingering in lines of poetry.

A moment where judgment lapses
but this time not for the wrong reasons.
He is taking the wrong turn
but ending up on the right road.

A misprinted atlas leading
to a better destination.

He was love before I knew
what love was supposed to be.

He was a wild dream
and he was dreaming of me.

All it took was one fingerprint.

A touch of your hand
upon my heart

to awaken the glimmer
of hope

that once resided in my soul.

Restoring the confidence
that love could happen

a possibility

Bringing forth a silver lining
to the pain once endured.

I am free again at last.

And all it took was the right touch.

All it took was you.

Cheyenne Sioux 67

I saw you and my heart unfurled
like a field of wildflowers
seeing sunlight for the first time.

Cheyenne Sioux

Sun-kissed seeds nestled beneath
an April shower bring blushing blossoms.

I could swear my cheeks
match their peony pink tones

For I have just revealed
while waiting in the rain

I to have begun to sprout
and my heart buds
to the beat of your name.

Call it spring fever
or whatever you may

but I'm smitten with you,

what else can I say?

Cheyenne Sioux   69

I planted roots in my dreamland
but you were ivy growing
in the crevices of my bones

You awakened me
to a garden sprouting within my soul.

Cheyenne Sioux

Sincerely Yours Forever, C.s.

We spent our summer days in the sun.

Brain freezes from melting ice cream
when I wore more than I ate

and belted out my favorite tunes
at the drive-in movies.

I had never felt so free to be myself
than each adventure with you.

And as I ride shotgun in your car
with our hands hovering close
and laughs in our smiles

I can't help but hope this lasts.

Because you have woken me
from the daydreams

and made me want to chase
reality instead.

Cheyenne Sioux   71

Sometimes love appears
like it ascended straight from heaven

and there is no time for your head
to catch up with your heart.

Cheyenne Sioux

I sensed it from the first moment,
the magic between us.

As you kissed me like dew kisses a rose

softly yet lingering

I somehow knew

you would always be mine.

There she stood
a beautiful, chaotic mess.

As the vines that grew
around her heart
    began to unravel.

For she had found someone
who saw past the thorns

and woke the sunlight
    in her soul.

Now her heart is filled
with buds

blooming at the sound
of his name.

Cheyenne Sioux

I grew a flower garden in my soul

What a beautiful thing
nurturing your heart can do.

Like moths to a flame
we were drawn to the other.

Dancing between eloquent stares
and melodious heartbeats

I found comfort
in the tender company we keep.

Like a serenity of swans
gracefully gliding by the water's edge

You took my hand and pulled me close
and I swore for a moment I was dreaming.

For I have never been one
to believe in fairytales.

But as nostalgia breathed into the air –

Cheyenne Sioux

Sincerely Yours Forever, C.s.

I could almost sense that
time had slowed, stilling to a halt.

Waiting for the moment
you and I realized –

We are timeless

and this love, has always been
and always will be,

written in the pages
of our many lifetimes.

Cheyenne Sioux

Your heart is a beautiful place
tangled with roses
      waiting to bloom.

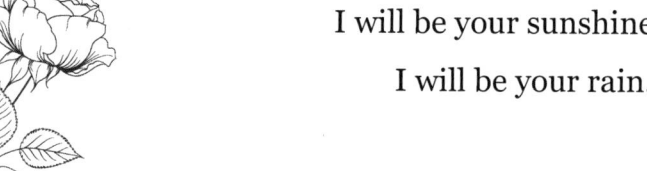

      I will be your sunshine
        I will be your rain.

Pouring all of my love
into the growth of you.

My love for him is not linear
it cannot be contained
within the margins of my pages

no matter how many times I try
in fear of being too much.

It is free, *expansive*, and ever-changing

— *This love is poetry in its truest form.*

I saw that glisten in your eye

and I knew we were

thinking the same

How does one get so lucky

to simply *breathe* the others name?

Cheyenne Sioux

I grabbed parchment and a pen
staining ink upon the pages
trying to find the words
to say my heart is

sincerely yours.

Cheyenne Sioux   81

Love is magical
the collecting of stardust
in the void between two souls

that slowly gravitate

c l o s e r

until eventually, they find
themselves caught in each other's orbit.

Cheyenne Sioux

Capture this moment
 with me, my darling.

For I wish to always remember
the very moment

when I knew
you were my one.

We took a polaroid.

I wake to the hum of his guitar

strumming gentle melodies,

that fills the room with sweet serenity.

Honey drops of maple

     and freshly brewed coffee

stir the air and carry me

     out of my drifting daze.

I leave behind the warm sheets

his button-up shirt still clinging to my skin

and I'm spinning like the angels.

This golden love, is heavenly.

A perfect mix of beauty and harmony

and I am high up in the clouds

composing the breeze

with golden arrows of my own.

Cheyenne Sioux

Sincerely Yours Forever, C.s.

Our love becomes a symphony
held in every beam of sunlight

warming the earth
in the colors of my soul.

And like the stars with the moon
I burn for him every moment
of every day.

Cheyenne Sioux   85

I have a million I Love You's
left to give.

I hope you don't mind
if I stay a while.

"How About a Lifetime?"

She dreamt of the light of the sun
and the blooming of the flowers
but fell in love with the depths of the moon,
the glistening of starlight.

Cheyenne Sioux   87

I succumb to the incandescent melody
of our butterfly heartbeats

and the efflorescent glow of the
magic cultivating between the two of us.

We're on the verge of collision
stopping traffic with the starlight in our eyes.

Our love is luminous like a moonlit glow
reflecting on a night's tide
that has just been awakened
by gravities pull.

I feel the satin touch of your
hand clasping with mine

And I know deep in the
crevices of my soul

that I would do anything
to hold to our starlight forever.

Cheyenne Sioux

Our love was powerful

it shattered stars dusting the skies

in glistening speckles of light.

She looked at them and smiled

"How else do you think

the constellations were formed?"

Cheyenne Sioux   89

The thousand splendid suns
that hide behind her walls
shone iridescently through the cracks

as he chiseled away at the barriers
of her heart.

But what he failed to realize
lied within these fragments of her soul

and the endless desire
to burn brightly only for him.

She was already infinitely his

and this light was the beacon
summoning him home at last.

Cheyenne Sioux

Two souls tethered so tightly even the moon
can't stop drawing them together.

A love more powerful than gravity

I melted the stars of the milky way
into the palms of my hands

And still, it wasn't enough
to signify the depth of our love.

For no moon, star, or outer space
could ever compare
to the tether, two souls can share

When their cosmic dust
collects and combusts;

a supernova awakening
as we gradually descend into love.

Cheyenne Sioux

Beneath the silhouette
of the moon's light

I am stardust

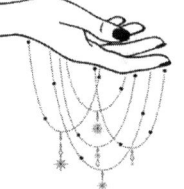

melting into the palm of your hands.

I lay down my armor
and find solace
in the moonlit melodies of your heart.

I let your words cascade over me
illuminating my soul
in the twinkle of the star's light

and the serenity of your presence
be what calms me

stills me

> *moves me.*

It's a delicate balance
this dance between you and me.

But there's something
in this moment

that keeps me returning
and laying down my armor once more.

Cheyenne Sioux

He brings me solace
whispering onto my skin,
like a satin robe upon my shoulders
I wear it proudly.

Unafraid of exposing my soul
I blossom in the moonlight
only for his love.

- An ode to vulnerability

"Don't you see?"

She spoke.

Loving you is starlight.

Even on the darkest of days
it will always be there
illuminating every piece of me.

I told the moon about you
and even it seemed to shine a little brighter.

Shades of dreamy nightfall,

amethyst and sea-foam,

litter the sky in starlight.

I feel the serenity wash over me

like the lulling whisper

of a siren's song

And find myself whispering

my own secrets to the sky.

I'm lost in the gravity of your love

and wish not to be found

but to burn brightly in your orbit.

It appears to me,

that I have learned

the secrets of the stars

And why they choose to shine so brightly

every night for the moon.

Cheyenne Sioux

I learned when you find the *right* love
it's better than any fairytale you could ever imagine.

Hold on tight, your ever after awaits you.

I've been asked why I write
and so, I'll tell you the reason why
for I have come to know the fears
from which away we all shy.

This is but a way
of making sense of who I am
and to show someone else
they have the strength to withstand.

If I can touch even a single person's heart
that for me is enough,
to watch them blossom into art.

Cheyenne Sioux

She wears a smile filled with sorrow
but eyes focused on her dreams
and this world may be brutal
but she is threading the future's seams.

This is but the beginning
of a never-ending tale
of the girl who was fated
to break her wings and fail.

And as you have seen she
has fallen before
but the strength she has found
fuels her heart enough to soar.

Cheyenne Sioux

With stardust in her soul

and moonlight in her eyes

she wrote them all a poem

across the darkened skies

and as she gazed into the night

the stars spelled out in a twinkling light

- Sincerely Yours Forever, C.S.

About the Author

Cheyenne Sioux is a twenty-seven-year-old writer and

poet from Virginia. She fell in love with poetry when it became a way for her to express her innermost thoughts and feelings and a way to decipher through the darkness in life and find the moonlight. Poetry has not only become her form of self- expression but a way for her to show others in this world that may be struggling with anxiety, depression, heartbreak, or hopelessness that there is still light and strength left within them. At the same time, her poetry also follows themes of encouragement, daydreams, and romance she aims always to be true to the feelings of her heart and a voice that resonates with a variety of experiences others are going through.

Her debut poetry book Sincerely Yours Forever, C.S. is a love letter to herself and others that even amidst the shadows you can uncover your greatness, find whom you are meant to be, and when it's time the love your heart aches for will come to light.

Cheyenne Sioux   103

Made in the USA
Middletown, DE
06 March 2023

26164331R00057